CW00403245

Kindness is magic!

Copyright of Jamie Hodges 2021

Dedicated to Jasper.
The best boy there is!

J.C was a fluffy, fun loving pup.

He loved to run around
and chase balls but most of all...

he loved
to play in the mud!

He would
dive in it,

he would
slide in it,

he would

splish and splosh and splash

in it!

One day, when he was

dunking and diving and digging

in the mud,

some
other puppies
saw him.

They began to laugh and point
and call him names.

they shouted.

This made J.C
terribly upset.

He did not know why they were being
mean; he was only having fun.

The next day
mummy dog asked
J.C if he was going
to play in the mud.

"Not today" J.C replied in
a low voice.

"Why not, is everything okay?"
mummy dog asked, concerned.

"The other pups made fun
of me for

in the mud" said J.C

Mummy dog hugged J.C tightly
and softly said,

"Do not be afraid to do
something you love. Others will
not always understand what or
why you are doing it. They might
also be scared to do it
themselves."

This made J.C feel much better.

Later that afternoon, J.C decided to play in the mud.

He did love it after all!

But soon, when he was covered from head to paw from all the

the other pups came around the corner.

They began to laugh and point again...

but this time J.C remembered
what his mum had said.

Bravely J.C called to them
"Did you want to play in
the mud too?"

They all laughed louder and harder and the biggest pup barked

"It's really fun!" replied J.C,

"especially when you

splish and splosh and splash

all over!"

Then, from behind the bigger pup, a smaller puppy peaked out

and with all his courage said, "I'll try!"

He ran towards the mud puddle and
with the biggest jump he could
muster dived in headfirst.

He did some

flipping and flopping and flumping

and was covered in mud!

He loved it!

"Come on guys!" he shouted to the other pups, "this is great!"

The other pups all ran as fast as they could and did their biggest dives.

The mud flew everywhere!

It was so much fun and they all
laughed together as they

splish, splosh, splashed

and

flip, flop, flumped

in the mud.

"You were right!"
said the big pup,
"this is brilliant,
bog dog!"

The next morning there was a knock at J.C's door. Stood there was the new gang,

"Is bog dog allowed out to play?"

they all asked eagerly.

J.C smiled the widest smile and
bounded out to play!

Printed in Great Britain
by Amazon

56327349R00015

SHORTS

Four short English plays by David Adair

Leaving Your Mark

Hobby Horse

All Change

Occupational Hazard

LEAVING

YOUR MARK